THE JAGS

The Team Talk

TOM WATT

RISING STARS

Rising Stars UK Ltd.
7 Hatchers Mews, Bermondsey Street, London SE1 3GS
www.risingstars-uk.com

Published 2009
Reprinted 2013

Publisher: Gill Budgell
Editor: Jane Wood
Text design and typesetting: Clive Sutherland
Illustrator: Michael Emmerson for Advocate Art
Cover design: Burville-Riley Partnership
Cover photograph: Ron Coello at www.coellophotography.co.uk
With special thanks to; Robert Dye, Harry Garner, Tyrone Smith, Lewis
McKenzie, Kobina Crankson and Alex Whyte

British Library Cataloguing in Publication Data.
A CIP record for this book is available from the British Library.

ISBN: 978-1-84680-483-0

Printed in the UK by Ashford Colour Press., Gosport, Hants

Contents

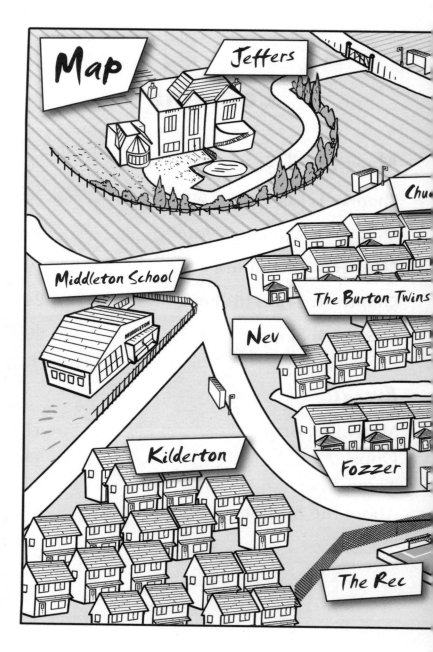

Meet the Jags

Andy

Name: Andrew Burton

Fact: He's the Jags' captain.

Loves: Spurs

FYI: The Jags may be his mates, but they'd better not forget he's the Skipper.

Burts

Name: Terry Burton

Fact: He's Andy's twin brother.

Loves: Football, football, and more football. He's football crazy!

FYI: He's a big Arsenal fan.

Dev

Name: Ryan Devlin

Fact: He's very forgetful.

Loves: Daydreaming!

FYI: He's always covered in mud and bruises.

Fozzer

Name: Hamed Foster

Fact: He can run like crazy, but he shoots like crazy too – sometimes at the wrong goal!

Loves: Telling bad jokes.

FYI: His best friend is Nev.

Keeps

Name: Jim Ward

Fact: He's the Jags' Number One goalie – whether he likes it or not!

Loves: Trying to score from his end of the pitch.

FYI: He's the tallest member of the Jags.

Jeffers

Name: Jeffrey Gilfoyle Chapman

Fact: He's the only one of the Jags who doesn't live on the Chudley Park estate.

Loves: Being in the Jags.

FYI: He's the Jags' top goal-scorer.

Name: Denton Neville

Fact: Nev is the Jags' most talented player.

Loves: Fozzer's bad jokes.

FYI: He keeps his feet on the ground and always looks out for his football crazy mates.

Name: Pam Burton

Fact: The Burton twins' mum, and a team 'mum' for all the Jags.

Loves: Sorting out her boys.

FYI: Doesn't actually like football!

Name: Jack Ward

Fact: He's Jim's dad and the Jags' coach!

Loves: Going on and on, doing his team talks.

FYI: He's taking his coaching exams.

8

① Lucky To Get Nil

> Fields Road are a good team. But even so, we shouldn't have been 1–0 down after five minutes. And it got worse. Me and Keeps got in a muddle, and let in their striker. We were 2–0 down!

Keeps Why did you try to pass back, Andy? Did I call for the ball?

Andy I had nobody to pass to, did I?

Keeps   Well, you could have put it out for a throw.

Andy   But that's not football. Your dad always tells us to play our way out of danger.

Keeps   Yeah. But not if it's going to lose us the game. I had no chance of getting that.

What's going on? Keeps is one of my best mates and here we are arguing. I'll talk to him later.

Keeps   Well we only lost 3–0, Skipper. It could have been worse.

Andy   Maybe. But so what? We still lost, didn't we?

Keeps   There's always next week. You can't get too down.

Andy   You're right. But I get so worked up, being captain. Look, I'm sorry I shouted at you.

11

Keeps   Well, I shouted at you first.
It was just a mix-up.

Andy   Yeah. But we don't have to lose
our tempers, do we?

Keeps   Well, you see lots of top players
losing their tempers during
games.

Andy   But it's their job. They have to win games and cups. We're just supposed to be having fun.

Keeps   We *are* having fun. Playing for the Jags is the best thing going, isn't it?

Andy   I don't know. I'm just fed up at losing like that!

Armchair Fans

Andy loves football. So I couldn't believe how fed up he was about losing. I went round to see him later on.

Keeps Hi, Andy. What's up?

Andy Oh, I don't know. I just hate losing and it feels like my fault.

Keeps   Try to forget it. Why don't we
        watch Spurs against
        Middlesbrough on TV?

Andy   Yeah, okay.

Andy   Thanks for the crisps, Keeps.

Keeps   No problem, Andy.

Andy   Spurs are looking good.

Keeps   You always say that. But I bet
              Middlesbrough will beat them.
              They always do at home.

Andy Don't say that. Or you can have your crisps back and go home!

Keeps Hold on! We're not going to argue again, are we?

Andy No. I'm only joking. But don't wind me up. This is a big game for Spurs. So it's a big game for me, too.

Everybody knows Andy's mad about Spurs. Sometimes I wish I had a team I was a fan of like that. Then again, who wants to be that nervous watching TV?

Keeps   Okay, but don't forget, watching a big game is supposed to be big fun!

All Square

In fact, Spurs against Middlesbrough was a good game. And I liked watching with Andy. He kept going: "Ooh!" and "Aah!" It was like being in the crowd.

Andy   Getting a 1–1 draw is better than nothing, but we should have had all three points, Keeps.

Keeps   What do you mean, "we"? I was just watching the game.

Andy   I know. But if you're watching with me, then you have to support Spurs! That first goal was brilliant, wasn't it?

Keeps   I suppose so. But what about Middlesbrough's goal?

Andy   Yeah. I don't know what our lot were doing. The defender and the goalie should have been talking to each other.

Keeps   Yes, like we should have been talking to each other, when we let that goal in against Fields Road!

Andy   Well, if the top players can have that kind of mix-up, then we can too!

Keeps   But the Spurs players didn't have a big argument like us, did they?

Andy   No. But maybe they'll sort it out in training.

Keeps   That's what we should have done, sorted it out in training. Football's fun, but arguing about it isn't.

Andy   Yeah. We should be helping each other when things go wrong, not arguing. Come on, let's go out in the garden and play. You be in goal. I'll be David Bentley taking free kicks.

So we did. But we did some more talking as well!

Call This Fun?

Me against Andy really is fun! Or should I say, me against David Bentley ...

Andy   And Bentley lines this one up ...

Keeps   You're too close! Do you want to knock my head off?

Andy   The goalie is moaning to the ref but that won't put Bentley off. He steps up.

Keeps   I'm David James now, by the way.

Andy   No goalie in the world will stop this one, Keeps. Bang!

Keeps   What a save! James dives to his left and gets a hand to it!

Andy Okay, let's have a break. Mum's got a drink for us.

Keeps Thanks, Mrs Burton.

Andy Yeah, thanks Mum. I need this.

Keeps Where's your brother today, Andy?

Andy   He was fed up after the game because we were arguing. He's gone round to Fozzer's.

Keeps   I suppose it's no fun watching us argue.

Andy   No. But it's only because we want to win. And we blame each other when things don't work out.

Keeps It's not much fun when that happens, though, is it?

Andy I know. We play football for fun but then we want to win as well.

Keeps Yeah, but we want to stay mates too, don't we? Anyway, I've got to get home. I'll see you after school tomorrow. Bring a ball to kick around at lunchtime!

Skipper

Training was a laugh in the week.
Mr Ward told us not to worry about
losing to Fields Road. But then he made
us hop all round the pitch to make up for
it! I told Keeps that I wanted to do a
team talk for Sunday's game.

Keeps   What are you going to say,
Skipper?

Andy I don't know yet. But I want to make sure we have fun *and* win.

Keeps I don't know what you can say to make that happen. But good luck!

Andy   Thanks. Promise you won't try to put me off by mucking about?

Keeps   I promise. Unless you make me laugh. Or Fozzer tells one of his jokes!

I'm the Jags' captain and I love playing for the team. I didn't want us to have another game like the last one. So, on Sunday, I stood up in the changing room before the game.

Keeps   Quiet, lads. I think Andy's got something to say.

Andy   Thanks, Keeps. Well, you all know what happened last Sunday. We can't let that happen again.

Keeps   Yeah. Sorry, Andy.

Andy   No, Keeps. It was my fault, too. We just have to remember that, no matter how much we want to win, we're mates. If we lose, we're still mates. But because we're mates, we can win!

We felt good as we ran out on to the pitch. But then a corner came over. I missed the ball. It hit Andy on the head and went in. We were losing 1–0! Andy looked at me. I looked at him. The rest of the team looked at both of us.

Andy Bad luck, Keeps.

Keeps Sorry, lads. My fault.

Andy What do you mean? It was *me* that scored the own goal!

Keeps   Yeah. Unlucky, Skipper. But remember, even Spurs players make mistakes sometimes. It's only 1–0. There's plenty of time to get back into the game.

Andy   Yeah. We can still win this.

Keeps   And still be mates, too! Come on, Jags!

We played really well for the rest of the half. And my brother made it 1–1.

Keeps Great goal, Burts.

Andy Yeah, not bad for an Arsenal fan, Burts!

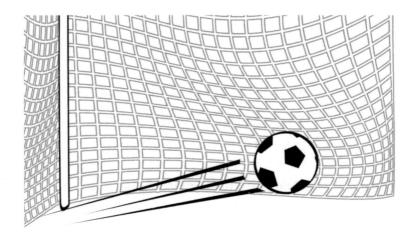

Keeps   Come on, Jags. Let's have some
fun and get another goal! I'll
kick it out to you, Skipper.

Andy   Good ball, Keeps. And now Nev's
made a run into the box. Can I
find him with a pass?

Keeps   What a goal! What a pass, Andy! What a finish, Nev!

Andy   Your kick out started it, Keeps. Look what happens when we tell each other what we're going to do!

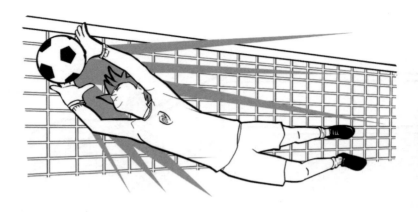

Keeps   Well, I'm going to save every shot that comes my way now. That's what I'm going to do!

And he did, too! We won 2–1 and it was one of the best games ever. It was fun because we won. But maybe we won because we had fun.

Keeps   Brilliant! Well, played, Skipper.

Andy   Well played, everyone. Who was man of the match? I'd say it was Keeps!

Keeps   Team spirit won it, Skipper. Or maybe it was your team talk.

Andy   Well, I hope we won't need a
            team talk next week. I'm sure we
            won't need one if we keep
            playing like that!

Keeps   We are the Jags!
and Andy

MIDDLESBROUGH 1 SPURS 1

Andy's right. When we play football, sometimes we argue. But it's not just us. Star players do it as well. Like that game we watched round at his house. It was going well for Spurs at first.

Andy   Oh, yes! It's 1–0 to Spurs. The goalkeeper never had a chance.

Keeps   I don't know about that, Andy.
I think he just couldn't see.

Andy   Exactly! No chance. That curl
on the shot fooled him, too.

Keeps   Only five minutes left now,
Andy.

Andy   I know. Will we hang on?

Keeps   Well, Spurs need to get it up the
other end of the pitch.

Andy   Come on, Spurs!

Keeps   Oh, no! Disaster! The keeper
and the full back have both left
it for each other.

Andy   I can see that, can't I?

Keeps   Well, don't blame me. That's
1–1. A draw is better than a
defeat, isn't it?

Andy   Maybe, Keeps. But it doesn't feel
like that at the moment!

Oops!

Football is about skill and tactics and great goals. But that's not all. It's about mistakes as well. Sometimes, one mistake can decide a game.

Sometimes a player makes a mistake. Sometimes team-mates get mixed up. Sometimes the manager picks the wrong team. Sometimes the referee gives a penalty when it was a fair tackle.

 Sometimes a player or the referee make mistakes. People often make mistakes in a game because they are worrying too much.

 When you make a mistake and a goal goes in, you have to forget it. You can always talk about it later. You need to think about what is happening next, not about what has just happened. The other team might make a mistake and let you back in the game!

Team Quiz

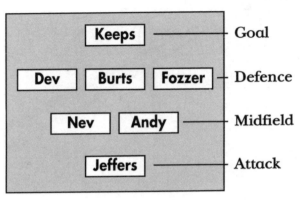

Keeps			— Goal
Dev	**Burts**	**Fozzer**	— Defence
Nev	**Andy**		— Midfield
Jeffers			— Attack

Questions

1 Who's in goal for the Jags?

2 What is Jeffers' job?

3 Who are the Jags' defenders?

4 Where do Nev and Andy play?

Answers

1 Keeps.

2 Striker/attacker.

3 Dev, Burts and Fozzer.

4 Midfield.

About the Author

Tom Watt tried not to make any mistakes when he wrote the Jags books. He used to make lots of mistakes when he played football, though! He used to score own goals sometimes. He would miss tackles. He'd bump into his own players.

Tom didn't let his mistakes worry him, though. He kept trying to get better at football. But now it's a bit too late. He's too old to play these days. That's why he writes books about football instead!

THE JAGS

Who's Got My Boots?
A New Striker
The Derby Match
Who's Washing the Kit?
The Big Deal
Star Player Wanted
Your Turn in Goal
The Team Talk
Whose Side Are You On?
Hitting the Headlines
Up for the Cup
The Own Goal

RISING★STARS

The Jags books are available from most book sellers.
For mail order information
please call Rising Stars on 0800 091 1602
or visit www.risingstars-uk.com